WELCOME TO
PASSPORT TO READING
A beginning reader's ticket to a brand-new world!

Every book in this program is designed to build read-along and read-alone skills, level by level, through engaging and enriching stories. As the reader turns each page, he or she will become more confident with new vocabulary, sight words, and comprehension.

These PASSPORT TO READING levels will help you choose the perfect book for every reader.

READING TOGETHER
Read short words in simple sentence structures together to begin a reader's journey.

READING OUT LOUD
Encourage developing readers to sound out words in more complex stories with simple vocabulary.

READING INDEPENDENTLY
Newly independent readers gain confidence reading more complex sentences with higher word counts.

READY TO READ MORE
Readers prepare for chapter books with fewer illustrations and longer paragraphs.

This book features sight words from the educator-supported Dolch Sight Words List. This encourages the reader to recognize commonly used vocabulary words, increasing reading speed and fluency.

For more information, please visit passporttoreadingbooks.com.

Enjoy the journey!

Cover design by Ching Chan.

Little, Brown and Company
Hachette Book Group
1290 Avenue of the Americas, New York, NY 10104
Visit us at LBYR.com

First Edition: March 2019

Little, Brown and Company is a division of Hachette Book Group, Inc.
The Little, Brown name and logo are trademarks of Hachette Book Group, Inc.

The publisher is not responsible for websites (or their content) that are not owned by the publisher.

Library of Congress Control Number 2018955214

ISBNs: 978-0-316-48740-5 (pbk.), 978-0-316-48743-6 (ebook), 978-0-316-48739-9 (ebook), 978-0-316-48744-3 (ebook)

Printed in the United States of America

CW

10 9 8 7 6 5 4

Passport to Reading titles are leveled by independent reviewers applying the standards developed by Irene Fountas and Gay Su Pinnell in *Matching Books to Readers: Using Leveled Books in Guided Reading*, Heinemann, 1999.

OFFICIAL
MARK OF
SPIRIT

DREAMWORKS

Spirit

RIDING FREE

Meet the PALS

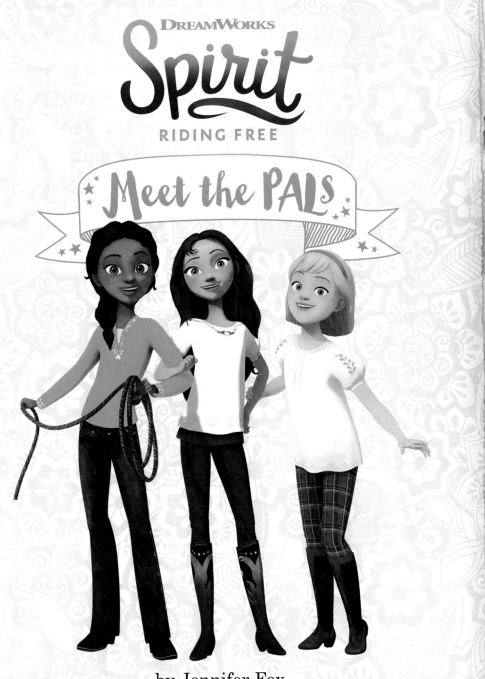

by Jennifer Fox

LITTLE, BROWN AND COMPANY
New York   Boston

Attention, Spirit Riding Free fans!
Look for these words
when you read this book.
Can you spot them all?

home

friends

ride

horse

Meet Lucky.

She is moving from a big city
to a small town named Miradero.

Lucky

Lucky rides a train to town.

Will she like her new home?

Lucky goes to school.

It is her first day.

She wears a fancy dress.

The other kids give her
funny looks.

Being new is hard.

Lucky has no friends here.

She eats lunch alone.

Soon Lucky makes new friends.

"I am Pru," a girl says.

Pru

"And I am Abigail.
Do you want to come
riding with us?"

Abigail

Pru's dad has a horse ranch.

Pru and Abigail are great riders.

Pru's horse is named
Chica Linda.

Abigail's horse is named
Boomerang.

Lucky likes horses,
but she does not know
how to ride.

Lucky meets a horse
named Spirit.

Spirit is wild.
No one can ride him.

Lucky knows Spirit is special.

"Hey there," she says gently.

Spirit likes Lucky, too.

Spirit lets Lucky ride him.

"Whoa, boy!" she says.

"Slow down!"

Lucky can ride with Pru and Abigail!

Later, Pru's dad says,
"Lucky, Spirit should be yours.
No one else can ride him."

Lucky loves Spirit,
but she cannot keep him.

She believes no one can own Spirit
because he is wild at heart.

So Lucky lets Spirit go.

"Good-bye, Spirit.

Be free," says Lucky.

Spirit runs through the hills.

But he is not gone for long!
Spirit loves Lucky and
comes back to her.

Lucky and Spirit can keep riding
with Lucky's new friends.

Together, **P**ru, **A**bigail, and **L**ucky
are the **PAL**s.

Their horses Chica Linda,
Boomerang, and Spirit
are pals, too.

"Come on, PALs!" Lucky calls.

These friends are always ready to ride off on an adventure.

Now Miradero feels like home.

There is no place
Lucky would rather be.

Lucky loves being here
with Spirit, riding free!